BY HER MAJESTY QUEEN RANIA AL ABDULLAH

The Sandwich Swap

with Kelly DiPucchio ❋ ILLUSTRATED BY Tricia Tusa

Disney • HYPERION BOOKS

NEW YORK

5 7 9 10 8 6 4
F322-8368-0-11063
Printed in the United States of America
This book is set in Goudy Italian
Display type is Tapioca
Designed by Judythe Sieck

Reinforced binding
Library of Congress Cataloging-in-Publication Data on file.
ISBN 978-1-4231-2484-9
Visit www.hyperionbooksforchildren.com

To Hussein, Iman, Salma, and Hashem:
my little ambassadors of hope . . . and to all the world's children:
swapping sandwiches is just the start.

—*Rania Al Abdullah*

For my best girlfriends—
Janie, Carolyn, April, Hope, Lisa, Paula, Susi,
Dawn, Jessica, Laura, and Lisa K.

—*Kelly DiPucchio*

For Judythe, thank you.

—*Tricia Tusa*

It all began with a peanut butter and jelly sandwich . . .

…and it ended with a hummus sandwich.

Salma and Lily were best friends at school.

They drew pictures together.

They played on the swings together.

They jumped rope together.

And they ate their lunches together.

But just *what* they ate was a little different.

Lily ate a peanut butter and jelly sandwich every day for lunch.

Salma ate a hummus and pita sandwich every day for lunch.

And although Lily never said it out loud,

she thought Salma's sandwich looked weird and yucky.

She felt terrible that her friend had to eat

that icky chickpea paste every day.

EW. Yuck.

And although Salma never said it out loud, *she* thought

Lily's sandwich looked strange and gross.

She felt just awful that her friend had to eat

that gooey peanut paste every day.

EW. Gross.

Then one day, Lily just couldn't hold back those pesky thoughts any longer.

"Your sandwich looks kind of yucky," she blurted out.

"What did you say?" Salma asked, thinking she must have misunderstood her friend.

"I *said*, your sandwich looks yucky."

Salma frowned. She looked down at the thin, soft bread, and she thought of her beautiful, smiling mother as she carefully cut Salma's sandwich into two neat halves that morning.

Her hurt feelings turned mad.

"Yeah, well your sandwich looks gross, and it smells bad too!" Salma snapped back.

Lily looked surprised. She sniffed the thick, squishy bread, and she thought of her dad in his silly apron, whistling as he cut Lily's sandwich into two perfect triangles that morning.

Lily scowled. "It does not smell bad!"

"Does too!"

"Ewww...YUCK!"

"Ewww...GROSS!"

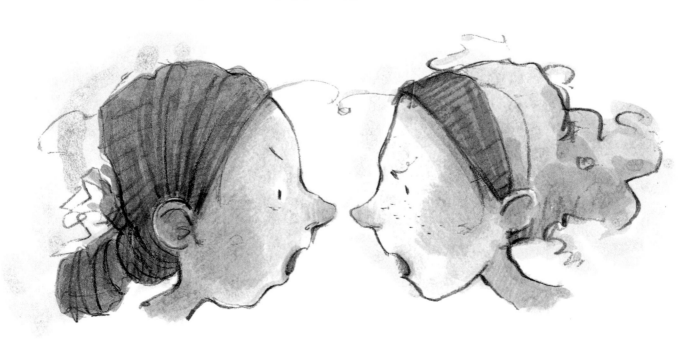

That afternoon the friends did not draw pictures
together. They did not swing together, and they did
not jump rope together either.

The next day, Salma ate her lunch at one table and Lily ate her lunch at another.

Meanwhile, the peanut butter vs. hummus story had spread, and everyone began choosing sides. Each side had something not so nice to say to the other.

Peanut butter breath!

Jelly heads!

Garlic breath!

Chickpea brains!

Pretty soon the rude insults had nothing at all to do with peanut butter or hummus.

You're weird!
You're STUPID!
You look funny!
You DRESS dumb!

And then it happened. Somebody yelled,

FOOD FIGHT!

Peanut butter and hummus sandwiches and other lunch favorites began flying back and forth between both sides of the lunchroom.

They stuck to the walls.

They stuck to the ceiling.

They stuck to the lunch lady.

When the sandwiches were all gone, pudding cups and applesauce and carrot sticks took flight.

Salma and Lily looked at one another from across the rowdy, splattered room.

They both felt ashamed by what they saw.

They both felt *really* ashamed
when the principal called them into
her office—after they had helped
clean up the mess.

The following day, Salma set her lunch down across from Lily's. The two girls nibbled on their sandwiches in silence. Finally, Lily got up the courage to speak. "Would you like to try a bite of my peanut butter and jelly?"

Salma grinned. "Sure. Why not? Would you like to try my hummus and pita?"

Lily laughed. "I'd like that."

"On the count of three?"

"Okay. On the count of three!"

1...2...3!

"Hey, this is *delicious*!"
"And this is *heavenly*!"
The girls giggled.
And hugged.
And traded sandwiches.

After lunch, Salma and Lily met with the principal again. This time
they were there to suggest a very special event for the whole school.

And *that's* how it all began with a
peanut butter and jelly sandwich...

... and ended with a
hummus and pita sandwich.

AUTHOR'S NOTE

When I was in nursery school, my mother used to send me off every morning with a hummus sandwich inside my lunch box.

One day, I watched a friend open *her* lunch box and bite into a peanut butter and jelly sandwich, and I thought—how revolting! I had never seen food so strange. She asked if I would like to try it and, because I didn't want to hurt her feelings, I braced myself and tasted it.

Well, I thought it was *heavenly.*

I learned a lesson that day and that's how this story came about.

It's easy to jump to conclusions when we come across something new or foreign or strange. But if we take the time to get to know each other, stand in each other's shoes, and listen to a different point of view, we learn something wonderful—about someone else and about ourselves.

I want every child who reads the tale of Salma and Lily to understand this. When they do, they'll each become a little ambassador of hope, someone who helps bring people of *all* cultures and backgrounds closer together.

—Rania Al Abdullah